The Solemn Sea

E. ROBERT BROOKS

Publishing Coordinator – Sharon Kizziah-Holmes

Paperback-Press
an imprint of A & S Publishing
Paperback Press, LLC.

ISBN -13: 978-1-960499-21-9

Semper Paratus

PROLOGUE

Despite the almost deafening cacophony from the fierce storm, we clearly heard Jean-Baptiste's skiff bang into the hull as he tied up alongside - the sound from the impact reverberated through the superstructure above us.

Coming aboard, he immediately sought shelter below from the howling, merciless wind and incessant, driving rain.

As he joined us in the salon, thoroughly drenched and looking like a bedraggled, soaked rat, he glared accusingly at the

Commander - with pent-up rage blazing like white hot coals in his normally impenetrable dark eyes.

Water dripped off his foul weather gear and formed a steaming puddle beneath him as he pulled off the encumbering garments.

With agitated invective in his voice, he accused the Commander of purposely placing him in harm's way by sending him into the treacherous tempest on a fool's errand!

Unruffled, the Commander observed in his typical roundabout, loquacious manner, "I may inadvertently give you bad advice from time-to-time, but rest assured I will never intentionally serve you bad liquor!"

To emphasize his point, he rummaged about in his sea chest and triumphantly hoisted a dusty old bottle of vintage 1939 dark Rhum from Martinique, labeled J. Bally des Plantations Lajus-du-Carbet.

A rare "navy strength" spirit, which we well knew he had purloined as an illicit memento from the boarding and seizure of a Columbian drug lord's yacht.

As he generously filled three heavy tumblers that had numerous small chips on the rims, accented by a conspiratorial wink, he quipped, "Smugglers distilled this."

Then, focusing his gaze on Jean-Baptiste, he retorted with masterful authority, "Once you have imbibed a sufficient quantity of this heady elixir, you can answer me with the respect befitting my rank, telling me everything you saw transpire on the miscreant's vessel!"

CHAPTER 1

The Commander was a well-respected and savvy Coast Guard veteran, a grizzled former officer, who during his early active-duty career piloted numerous combat zone landings of Marines off naval vessels onto war torn shorelines.

Upon his return to the United States during peacetime, he was assigned to south Florida, operating out of Sector Key West and stationed in Marathon.

Running an elite MSRT Direct Action Section (DAS) unit specializing in maritime counterterrorism and high-risk missions, he participated in numerous search and seizure operations.

He was born and raised along the southeast coast of Florida as a devout Southern Baptist to a family of fishermen who ran a small fleet of shrimp trawlers, and, unusually for a state with so many transients, had inhabited the region for several generations.

He first gained a taste for travel and adventure when he accompanied his parents on stints of missionary work in Africa and the Virgin Islands.

As a restless young man hungering for more than the limited options his family business and the local culture provided, he enlisted and took full advantage of the myriad training and educational opportunities his service afforded.

Due to experiences in the military which broadened his horizons and exposed him to different influences than his somewhat insular upbringing, as well as, troubling remembrances of friends lost in battle, he eventually abandoned his religions admonitions against drinking alcohol, but his thirst for knowledge, which began with his childhood bible studies, continued.

Over the years with long assignments at sea, he became a voracious reader, developing an impressive vocabulary and oratory skills, which he used to good effect when addressing his subordinates.

Upon his retirement, he joined the Coast Guard Auxiliary and purchased a boat, which he documented (registered) for Auxiliary use, that he evocatively named - Ascending Angel; a restored 1948 wooden forty-six-foot Chris Craft cabin cruiser he bought cheaply at auction after it had been confiscated from Haitian drug-runners.

The former owners had "customized" it with larger engines, and what initially appeared to the discerning eye to be an odd, incongruous, and amateurish mix of fiberglass and wood embellishments cobbled onto the once stately teak construction, which were cleverly designed, and intended to improve seaworthiness and increase storage and fuel capacity.

The combination of materials, and an almost total absence of any metal hardware which at great expense had been replaced by carbon fiber cleats, light housings, and other fixtures, produced a weak radar signature, allowing the smugglers to operate virtually undetected in the depths of the night.

He appreciated these stealthy attributes conveniently facilitating his own unusual nocturnal maritime escapades.

Though officially retired, the Commander secretly perpetuated his former lawman persona and craving for action.

Under the cover of his Coast Guard Auxiliary duties, he covertly operated as a self-appointed vigilante on the high seas, unfettered by the rules and regulations previously encumbering him and his active-duty compatriots.

He surreptitiously developed an extensive network of intelligence and informants, both from backchannel contacts within the ranks of the Drug Enforcement Administration (DEA) and Coast Guard, as well as, with other well-connected and often colorful military and seafaring acquaintances.

CHAPTER 2

Early the next morning, in the aftermath of the torrential storm, the sun's reflection shimmered beguilingly on the rippling surface of the tranquil jade-colored water in the bay where we anchored.

Shining vivid and bright, dazzling, and enchanting; drawing us towards it, almost as if subliminally beckoning us to leave all our cares behind and venture forth towards enlightenment at the edge of the world.

This momentary introspective and wistful contemplation was abruptly interrupted by crass interlopers arriving on noisy jet skis.

They proceeded to gun their motors and steer erratically, sending up rooster tails of water glistening in the sunlight.

Seemingly unperturbed as some of them jumped into the water to swim, the Commander serenely waved and smiled, while under his breath confiding to us that he had chummed these waters the previous day to attract bull sharks.

The deceptively serene coastal flats of the Florida Keys are interspersed by small islands with stands of dense, tangled mangroves teeming with life lurking in their shadows, and beneath the surface of murky waters where dangerous predators await.

Raising anchor and traversing our route, we surreptitiously shadowed the vessel Jean-Baptiste had scrutinized the previous evening.

I observed long tendrils of moss, like tattered burial shrouds hanging from branches of the gnarled old trees, with unseen root structures extending out into the narrow channels, poised to penetrate hulls and sink unwary mariners.

Iguanas with bloated vivid green bellies were perched on branches, flicking their tongues, and devouring wild Marsh Hibiscus flowers as we passed by.

Narrow flattened areas on the otherwise impenetrable shoreline revealed trails where alligators hauled themselves out of the water to bask in the sun.

All the while, the persistent buzzing drone of insects filled our ears, sporadically interjected by the sounds of splashing fish as they leapt to satiate their constant hunger.

Our surveillance proved uneventful, though the Commander carefully noted the route in his diary and seemed satisfied.

Late that afternoon, quickening wind gusts with low-lying dreamsicle-colored cotton candy clouds clustered together on the horizon, rims aglow from reflected sunlight accentuating the brooding darkness within, tell-tale signs more rain showers were imminent.

Though tempted to linger and continue gazing at the awe-inspiring beauty, we adhered to our risk assessment training rules, and after updating the risk/reward score, surmised it prudent to head back and endeavor to outrun the rapidly approaching storm.

The sea calls out to those prepared to listen with spellbinding whispers on the wind interspersed with the plaintive cry of seagulls.

A siren's song of seemingly disparate, melancholy notes, yet harmonious and inspiring, luring us to throw caution aside, explore the rapture of her beauty, vigorous vitality, and hidden mysteries.

However, beneath her sometimes warm and radiant veneer, the sea is perpetually cold and heartless in her depths; poised to surge with faint warning into a deadly maelstrom, ensnaring the reckless and unprepared in her fatal embrace.

CHAPTER 3

The Coast Guard is the only military branch of the United States Armed Forces authorized to operate within the borders of our country.

In peacetime, it enforces domestic and international maritime law, but during times of war is under the direction of the United States Navy.

Though related to the Navy, and the Marines, the Coast Guard is not part of the Department of Defense.

Due to inexplicable political machinations, it was formerly under the jurisdiction of the Treasury Department until 1967, when it was transferred to operate under the auspices of the Department of Transportation.

It was subsequently made a part of the newly created Department of Homeland Security in 2003 which better aligned with the service's actual role and responsibilities.

Those duties include surface and air search and rescue operations, and various law enforcement tasks.

Most notably, the interdiction of drug smuggling and human trafficking activities, and the apprehension of offenders in those illicit trades.

Given the ongoing immense amount of nautical activity in south Florida and the Florida Keys, the Coast Guard's presence there is perpetually undermanned and underfunded.

Though they are not authorized to fulfill law enforcement authority, the Coast Guard Auxiliary (whose volunteer members are often former peace officers, security, and military personnel) is very active supporting their "gold-side" active-duty brethren at the "tip of the spear."

They act as a force multiplier in all other

respects with sea and air search and rescue first responder tasks, as well as, performing watchstanding and other duties, freeing up active-duty personnel to focus on the most critical missions and considerable criminal infractions.

As a practical matter, when "bad guys" are engaged in a nefarious act and are approached by an official looking vessel, they don't discern the difference between active-duty and auxiliary personnel.

This can leave the unarmed Auxiliarists in unexpected and precarious situations when, during the course of their patrols, they unknowingly come upon the scene of a crime and risk being attacked...

CHAPTER 4

The Florida Keys Brewing Company in Islamorada is a noted local attraction that opened to great acclaim in 2015 with a range of expertly crafted and well-regarded beers.

One of their proprietary recipes, named Iguana Bait Kolsch, is made with local Keys honey and hibiscus, despite the German purity law strictly mandating traditional Kolsch only be made using barley, hops, water, and yeast.

This carefree, bending of the rules attitude, perhaps unknowingly, perpetuates a long tradition in the area.

Since discovery and subsequent settlement, unsavory denizens of South Florida and the Florida Keys from all levels of social strata have been responsible for a sometimes-colorful legacy of illegal activities to their financial benefit, including the trafficking of various contraband and undocumented illegal aliens, to, and from the area.

A long coastline with a multitude of small islands and waterways, in close proximity to the Bahamas, as well as other Caribbean islands and South America, have provided ideal commodity access, sea passages, and terrain for the smugglers to operate, making their apprehension difficult.

In more recent times, they augmented their route options and increased efficiency by using airplanes and makeshift landing strips.

Both the Seminole Wars and the American Civil War provided opportunities for unscrupulous individuals and factions to profiteer.

During the Cuban wars of independence in the 1800s, guns and supplies were smuggled into Cuba from Florida to fight the Spanish.

Throughout Prohibition in the 1920s and early 1930s, running rum from Cuba was a lucrative, albeit illegal, business.

Mirroring the transition by criminal elements in other parts of the country, in the 1960s and 1970s marijuana became the commodity of choice for smugglers who used hidden airfields and took advantage of the same remote waterways their bootlegging predecessors successfully used.

Then cocaine became popular in the 1980s, which resulted in even greater illicit profits and evolved the process for both the criminals and law enforcement personnel.

Federal and State Law Enforcement, who had previously been somewhat laconic, declared a "War on Drugs" and expanded their search and seizure capabilities in a futile effort to stop the smuggling.

The smugglers adapted, utilized sophisticated methods of transportation, including boats with hidden compartments, and submersibles, while adopting weapons with increased firepower and lethality, resulting in heightened violent encounters between law enforcement, and various gangs competing for dominance.

CHAPTER 5

Despite extensive and precise rules with rigorous checks and balances to monitor and enforce them, as in any service there exists in the Coast Guard isolated elements of corruption, and it is an unfortunate fact that not all Coast Guardsmen are benevolent and altruistic.

In 1988, fifteen Guardsmen in the Florida Keys, assigned to the Islamorada station and in cahoots with cocaine smugglers, were exposed during the "Operation Tempest" probe for sabotaging patrol boats, and selling information about secret law enforcement radio frequencies and codes.

One complicit Guardsman was murdered by his former accomplices when they learned he was being pressured to cooperate by federal investigators.

The mastermind of the perpetrators, however, proved to be elusive and was never publicly identified or prosecuted, although the Commander had suspicions about the identity of the ringleader.

Backchannel sources in the DEA, off the record informed the Commander of their prime suspect's name, Daniel Comin.

Like the Commander, Comin had been raised in south Florida in a seafaring and fishing family, but with a very different upbringing.

Taking after his parents, who were both petty criminals involved in occasional smuggling, what began as an indolent life as a ne'er-do-well, easily transitioned into an illicit career as an out-and-out con artist and charlatan.

From an early age he fell in with the notorious Barker crime family, however, unlike his parents, and due to his innate street smarts and cunning, he always managed to evade arrest.

The Barkers realized having a savvy "man on the inside" of local law enforcement would be significantly beneficial to their criminal enterprises.

They groomed Comin for a Coast Guard appointment using their considerable paid political influence to assure he advanced through the ranks.

In the Coast Guard, despite his vows to perform his duties professionally and ethically, unbeknownst to most of his compatriots, he provided regular reports to the Barkers on patrol schedules and investigation activities.

He ferreted out a multitude of opportunities to profiteer on the unfortunate and unwary, and, despite his outwardly engaging and compelling demeanor, he secretly lived by the adage: rules were made to be broken.

CHAPTER 6

The Barker Family had been in Florida for over one hundred years and were involved in narcotic smuggling in south Florida since the 1970s, transitioning from marijuana to cocaine and other drugs, then trafficking in illegal aliens.

Despite numerous arrests, they exploited inefficient and ineffective enforcement procedures, methods, and laws, allowing their criminal activities to thrive for decades.

Daniel Comin first met Richard and Ronald Barker working on fishing and shrimp trawlers owned by the Barker family.

As the Barker's criminal activities expanded, Comin learned the ropes of the drug and trafficking businesses, proving himself to be an able lieutenant.

By the time multiple elements of federal and state law enforcement shut down their operations, Comin was entrenched in the Coast Guard, escaping the casted net.

He struck out on his own, initially under the cover of his duties in the Coast Guard but biding his time to discreetly leave the service.

Once retired, he stayed involved in running drugs, but his focus became the clandestine ferrying of well-heeled illegal aliens from Nassau and Havana, to the Florida Keys, charging as much as $50,000 per person, including those with criminal records preventing them from entering the United States via more conventional means.

CHAPTER 7

S mugglers, illegal aliens, and law enforcement use all manner of boats to navigate the Florida waterways.

From rafts and cobbled together boats called Chugs used by refugees, to luxury cruisers, if it floats, someone has probably tried to adapt it to their need.

Stealthy one-hundred-foot narco semi-submersibles and submarines, multi-engine Cigarette, and other high performance racing style go-fast boats have been used by the drug trade, as well as, by their law enforcement adversaries.

Thirty-two to thirty-eight-foot multi-engine Picuda boats, mainly used by drug smugglers in the Caribbean, named after a tropical fish, are narrow, sleek, fast boats, that due to their low profile elude radar detection and cut through the waves.

Pangas, also called Yolas, are inexpensive twenty-six-to-thirty-foot, V-shaped hull boats which are fast and virtually un-sinkable.

They were originally intended for transporting fish, but became popular with Mexican drug runners, especially along the Baja coast of California.

The Pangas were initially made from wood, then fiberglass, pioneered in the early 1970s by an American builder named Mac Shroder, who was from Barrington, Illinois.

CHAPTER 8

The Commander first encountered Daniel Comin when they were both serving in the Coast Guard in Florida and involved in a two-boat training drill off Station Islamorada.

From the very first impression, the Commander sensed something disingenuous and bent about Comin.

He innately disliked Comin's overly folksy manner and brash confidence, accented by an intentionally booming voice and bravado which came across like the pitch line of a bad used car salesman, or a blatant flimflam swindler.

Even more troubling, in the Commander's estimation, Comin exuded an irritating self-absorbed demeanor; a need to constantly posture and prove his importance at the potential expense of the well-being of his crew and the rules intended to safeguard them.

The Commander silently vowed to keep an eye on Comin, and when the "Operation Tempest" scandal broke, through his sources he heard rumors of Comin's possible involvement and malfeasance, but Comin was never officially accused or arraigned.

Time passed with no revelations about Comin to support his concerns, and when Comin retired a few years later, he forgot about him and focused on duties elsewhere.

Eventually, the Commander also officially retired, and to implement his private crusade to surreptitiously continue to track down drug runners and human traffickers, he convinced Jean-Baptiste and me, who were already in the Auxiliary and had previously served in his MSRT DAS unit, to join him in this quest.

Prior to joining MSRT, I was a Coast Guard rescue swimmer, and Jean-Baptiste had served in a Hitron unit as a sniper who specialized in shooting the engines on go-fast drug boats from pursuing helicopters.

We succeeded to "under the radar" bring down several major criminal networks without revealing our role in their undoing to the arresting authorities, or the public.

In 1999, Comin came to the Commander's attention again when we participated in "Operation Sundown" in Key West as "off the books" undercover agents, and he was alleged by an informer to be involved.

Run by a combination of DEA agents, U.S. Customs, and Key West police, the stated mission goal was to rid the area of all illegal drug activity.

Over twenty suspects were arrested, and the officers confiscated large amounts of cocaine, crack, and ecstasy (MDMA), along with firearms; Comin yet again evaded capture.

CHAPTER 9

In addition to the interdiction of banned substances and animals, law enforcement in America contends with the influx of illegal aliens.

Throughout our history, smugglers have trafficked humans for slave labor and prostitution, also taking advantage of some refugees' ability to pay exorbitant amounts of money for safe passage.

These days, our media's primary illegal alien focus is on the United States' southern border along the Rio Grande.

However, Florida has a long history of

contending with the problem of illegal aliens, continuing into the present day, with alarming increases mirroring the exponential growth at our southern border, most notably with refugees from Cuba, Haiti, and the Dominican Republic.

Though not well publicized, since Russia invaded Ukraine, more than four million residents have fled their country, with some resettling in the United States.

Thousands of Russians have also left their homeland to escape economic sanctions and their governments oppressive crackdown on domestic dissent against the war.

Some of these refugees made their way through Mexico to our southern border in hopes of being granted asylum, but others with the financial wherewithal to afford it, traveled to Cuba with the plan to then come furtively to America.

One of the criminals in Florida who saw an opportunity to profit from their misfortune was Daniel Comin...

CHAPTER 10

There is some controversy about what rank Vladimir Putin actually held in the KGB at the time of his retirement from the service in 1991 to pursue a career in politics.

He publicly claimed to hold the rank of lieutenant colonel, but some sources allege he was a year away from attaining this rank and was merely a major.

What is certain though is his being a foreign intelligence officer for sixteen years, with a reputation for being both shrewd and utterly ruthless.

In March of 2022, Putin primarily focused on continuing his strategy for the invasion and occupation of Ukraine, initiated the previous month, but he was also aware the southern border of the United States had become an increasingly leaky sieve through which Mexican drug cartels were inserting their sicarios with impunity, and the Chinese Communist Party had penetrated spies disguised as refugees for future critical infrastructure sabotage missions.

He, therefore, hatched and authorized a plan to take advantage of this opportunity and infiltrate one of his most trusted agents, the scion of a high-ranking Politburo family named Dmitry Sechin, into America to carry out a plot he had nurtured for several years, code named "Climbing Bear."

His intent was to upset the U.S. governmental hierarchy with a quick surgical strike, and in the temporary power vacuum be able to facilitate his goals more easily and quickly for further conquest: expansion in eastern Europe, a return to Soviet glory, and global dominance.

Sechin would join a group of well-to-do expat refugees displaced by the Ukraine war, but rather than enter the United States through Mexico, he would be inserted into Florida from Havana.

On a Sunday afternoon in April of 2022 a sport-fishing boat captained by Daniel Comin departed Cuba and headed to Key West.

His passengers were well-dressed refugees from Russia and other Eastern European countries who had paid him handsomely to be illegally brought to America.

Upon arrival at the dock, they disembarked and most of them nonchalantly sauntered over to the famous Southernmost Beach Café to share drinks to celebrate their arrival.

The owner of the café was a longtime resident and had seen his share of illegal aliens through the years, though not so tourist-like and obviously affluent.

From the privacy of his office, he called the local police who in turn notified the Department of Homeland Security.

The group at the bar was taken into custody by U.S. Customs and Border Patrol agents, but Comin had already departed by sea, and the other occupants from the boat, most believed to have been from Russia, had also left the area before the border patrol officers arrived at the scene, and they successfully eluded capture.

Sechin had separated himself from the other fugitives and was driving to Islamorada in a nondescript car which had been waiting for him with carefully prepared forged identity documents in the glove compartment.

He would meet Comin again that evening at their prearranged location to progress the second phase of his plan...

CHAPTER 11

That afternoon, Jean-Baptiste and I received a request from the Commander to meet him at the Hog Heaven Sports Bar and Grill in Islamorada before our scheduled patrol.

Unbeknownst to us, the Commander had used his vast network of resources to have Comin's boat monitored by an ex-U.S. Navy P-3 Orion maritime patrol aircraft, converted to a so-called P-3 Long Range Tracker.

The surveillance plane operated out of Cecil Field, near Jacksonville, Florida, and was outfitted with APG-66V X-band pulse doppler radars, originally designed for F-16 fighter aircraft.

It also had SeaVue marine search radars and a suite of electro-optical sensors including night vision, digital zoom, and video recording capability.

The pilot had stealthily tracked Comin along his route from Cuba to Key West, and then to Islamorada.

When we met at the bar, across the room we saw Comin and an out-of-place looking pale-skinned stranger seated and talking together in earnest.

The bartender recognized the Commander and offered to comp us a round of drinks, but the Commander declined, explaining our imminent departure for a patrol.

The bartender suggested a raincheck, but while the offer was doubtlessly well-intentioned, and meant in earnest, we knew it was a requisite pleasantry, soon to be forgotten, and likely never to come to fruition.

Thanking him, we departed and made our way to the dock and the Commander's boat where we completed the dockside preparations for our patrol.

CHAPTER 12

With our previous military experience, the Commander, Jean-Baptiste, and I easily qualified with the Coast Guard Auxiliary for nighttime patrol certification.

Our stated training mission for the evening had been approved by the Order Issuing Authority (OIA), and the forecast was for a clear evening with normal conditions.

So, unless the risk assessment for the patrol changed, we would only need to check-in with the station watchstander by radio every 30 minutes while under way.

We assumed Comin's vessel would be outfitted with top-of-the-line radar and surveillance equipment, radio scanners, and that he knew the Coast Guard frequencies and codes.

Using paper charts to calculate and plot our course, we dead reckoned our line of travel without the use of GPS electronic navigation equipment or radar, which could be tracked and monitored.

With my luminous watch, I timed the legs of our proposed route, just as if we were executing a search and rescue pattern.

We proceeded otherwise radio silent, all lights now extinguished, relying solely on experience, visible aids to navigation channel markers and buoys, and the high resolution FLIR thermal imaging camera display at the helm.

Especially at night, the need for intense concentration to maintain constant vigilance when piloting a vessel, or acting as a lookout, can lead to tunnel vision, and what is colloquially described as "losing the bubble."

We didn't know when Comin would be leaving the bar, so we brought plenty of strong coffee, which, though it tasted acrid and bitter, served the purpose to keep us alert.

Though we did not follow it, according to the plan we had filed with the station, our first landmark was the shadowy skeletal remains of the Sombrero Key lighthouse off Marathon, which like the other five lighthouses in the Keys had been decommissioned and abandoned in 2015 by Coast Guard order, when costs for maintenance became prohibitive, and newer technology superseded.

Its once bright beacon had been a solitary sentinel incessantly reaching out in the gloomy night, striving to pierce inky darkness and dense fog to warn of the jagged reefs hidden just beneath the undulating waters.

In the distance, the muffled constant clanging of a ship's bell alerted us and other seafarers to its presence in the heavy mists further out to sea.

While we waited for Comin to depart, we whiled away the time - listening to the Commander recite historical seafaring anecdotes, of which he knew in inexhaustible abundance.

He related the term "larboard," for the loading side of a vessel (opposite of the steering side), was changed to port by decree of the British and American navies in the mid-1800s because the verbal commands enunciated in often windy and noisy conditions for larboard and starboard could be difficult to differentiate.

Eventually, commercial and pleasure boaters followed suit and adopted the same new directional naming convention.

Then he remarked how, inexplicably, in the United States, the maritime protocols for aids to navigation are not consistent from region-to-region.

Unprepared amateur captains coming in from areas such as the great lakes can experience disastrous accidents if they are only navigating visually, and not relying on GPS.

His reverie was interrupted when Jean-Baptiste alerted us from his lookout position that Comin's boat was pulling away from the dock.

I proceeded to join Jean-Baptiste in the bow with a large three-hundred-foot coil of gray-colored Sta-Set polyester line (rope for landlubbers) which would not float and be virtually invisible once cast into the water, and with its high abrasion resistance would be ideal for fouling Comin's props.

While the Commander steered a pattern back and forth over Comin's projected course, I quickly payed out the line.

Then the Commander headed away for four hundred yards and killed the engines so we could watch and hear the results of my mayhem.

Moments later, having cleared the harbor mouth Comin's boat increased speed until it came to a sudden halt accompanied by a mix of grinding, clunking, and rattling sounds.

I immediately called up the Coast Guard station on the radio, identifying our vessel three times per protocol, and informed the watchstander that we had encountered a vessel in distress, but that the coxswain had determined not to approach based on risk management assessment because it appeared to be a drug boat, and we needed immediate assistance from gold side active duty, or DEA.

Conveniently, there was a forty-five-foot Coast Guard boat in the area that arrived within ten minutes, fifty caliber machine guns visible and manned on the fore and aft

Sampson posts.

As they approached and hailed Comin's boat, their coxswain saluted us and motioned for us to accompany them.

We followed close astern and heard Comin swearing and splashing in the water as he tried in vain to free the props.

While one guardsman trained his machine gun on the floundering Comin, two others boarded the boat and searched it.

Sechin was brought up from below deck in handcuffs by one of them, while the other proceeded to offload several large packages of cocaine from one of our previous busts, Jean-Baptiste had kept for just such an occasion and hidden on the boat when Comin and Sechin were in the bar.

EPILOGUE

Per the station's request, while the active-duty boat processed the prisoners, we towed Comin's boat back to the harbor, and then after docking and securing it and our boat for the night, we reconvened at the bar for a nightcap.

The same bartender greeted us, and to our delight he remembered his promise and bought us a round of drinks!

We toasted and congratulated ourselves on the success of our covert mission, without even realizing at the time who Comin's passenger was.

Several days later, however, the Commander was summoned to a clandestine interview with a CIA agent, who it turned out he had ferried onto a wartime beach many years ago.

The agent discreetly briefed him about the sinister plot we had unknowingly thwarted, and that evening while we savored the last of the delectable 1939 Rhum, the Commander filled us in and swore us to secrecy.

Please enjoy the prologue of
The Latent Luthier

PROLOGUE

Billie Earl was a legendary session guitarist who had gotten his start in the Memphis Blues scene in the 1960s.

Moving to Nashville, he had been in high demand with local bands and regularly recorded with them.

He often performed at many well-known clubs and bars, but then one day he inexplicably vanished...

Until several years later, when he walked into Betty's Grill one night at 2:00am.

My friend, Jerry Eichhorn, and I were there with several other longtime patrons enjoying late after concert drinks and cheeseburgers.

When Billie had disappeared, for several months there had been widespread speculation around town about what had become of him.

Eventually, the gossip had died down, but Billie's fame persisted.

When he walked into the restaurant that night, one of the diners saw him, and yelled, "That's Billie Earl!", and everyone instantly recognized him.

The manager saw Billie, and we overheard her offer him a burger and a drink on the house, and though they would be closing in an hour, she asked if he would like to play a few songs.

Billie looked uncomfortable and replied that he didn't have a guitar with him.

Jerry chimed in on the conversation and offered to give him one of his to play.

Jerry was a third-generation luthier, or maker of stringed instruments.

The guitar he fetched from his truck exhibited a weathered patina, not from abuse, but due to extensive use over many years of play.

Billie scrutinized the pickups and switches of the unfamiliar "axe" and experimented with them to determine the range of settings.

At the same time, he ran the palm of his

left hand rapidly up and down the back of the maple neck several times, testing it for friction.

Plucking the strings, he momentarily frowned encountering the unexpected thickness of a wound G string, which was not conducive to his style of bending notes.

He tried different methods of articulating sound from the instrument, eventually nodding in satisfaction.

When Billie plugged into and turned on an amplifier, his fingers flittered over the strings as they wove an intricate and enticing musical pattern.

His audience were initially enraptured by the compelling tempo.

Then, the quickening cadence abruptly dissipated into a drawn-out melancholy sound with disparate tones...

It was an ethereal and complex creation, that, for no apparent reason, reminded me of a gossamer spider's web shimmering in reflected pale sunlight.

This unexpected vision sent a chill down my spine and seemed to whisper reminders of troubling childhood experiences.

The imaginary web almost imperceptibly undulating in the illusion of a faint breeze...

What was his inspiration for this haunting melody, I wondered?

What tribulations had contributed to this erratic soul-searching style of play?

Perhaps memories of the demise of a cherished loved one, or a lost muse from his past who had left invisible scars on his heart evoking emotions expressed through musical compositions?